# LOU

## Breanna Carzoo

**HARPER**
*An Imprint of HarperCollinsPublishers*

ISBN 978-0-06-305405-9

23 24 25 26  RTLO  10 9 8 7 6 5 4

❖

First Edition

To Chris, for seeing greatness in me
before I saw it in myself

# Hello!

## Can you see me down here?

My name is Lou, and I'm...

# a toilet.

All day,

every day,

one by one...

they **SNIFF**

and **TWIRL**

and **TWIST**

and **LIFT**

and...

well, you know.

I know I'm useful.

It's just that sometimes...

deep down inside,

I feel like there's more in me than what they can see.

Like I'm full of greatness!

I just don't know what it is

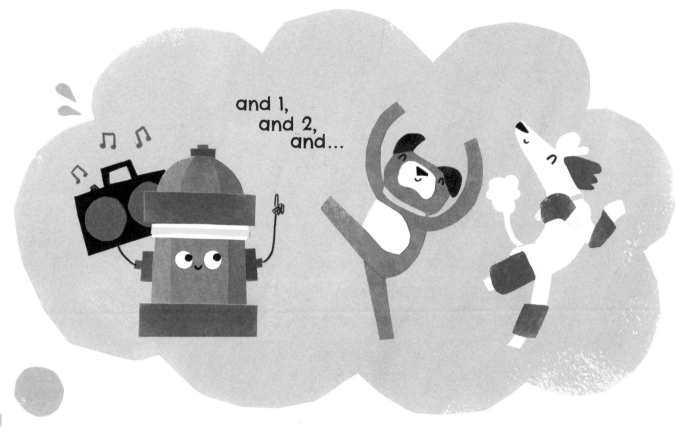

or how to let it out.

And can I tell you something?
Just between you and me?

I worry sometimes.

What if this is all I am? All I'll ever be?

What if I never do anything more...

...important?

Oh no, here we go again.

One by one, they...

# SNIFF and

Uh, do I see smoke?

# TWIRL and

Wait! What's going on?

# TWIST and

Whoa, that feels really weird.

# LIFT!

# Ah! Why's everyone looking at me?

Oh! I see it now!
I know what I have to do!

How did I not see this before?
My name is Lou, and I'm...

a superhero!